VOLUME 1

# Silly Nomads™

## From Palmerston Close

By M. E. Mohalland and J. L. Lewis
Illustrated by Kate Santee

MOHALLAND LEWIS LLC

ISBN 978-0-9897106-0-2

To my dad, Everald, whom I
affectionately call "Jomfeh," whose
inspiring words have helped steer me
on the right path,

To my grandmother, whom I
affectionately call "Mama,"

To my brother, Dain and his family,

And to all of my family in America
and in Jamaica.

~ Marcus

To my granddaughter, Lily,
whose energetic and creative spirit
has been my inspiration.

~ Jan

# Silly Nomads from Palmerston Close

# CONTENTS

# CHAPTER 1

# Wake Up Nomads

**B**ang, bang...*KA-BONG!* The sound of pots and pans falling out of the cupboard startled Suhcrom. He popped an eye open, but he was too drowsy to fully wake up.

*Ka-plop, ka-plop, ka-plop, ka-plop.* Naddih clomped across the floor, carrying a sack along with him. The clunky footsteps suddenly got louder and louder, and closer and closer. *Plunk*...he dropped the sack on the floor next to the couch.

"Oh, what is...?" Suhcrom dragged his head off the pillow and struggled to open his eyes. "Ahh!" He gasped. Naddih was just inches from his face, staring at him.

"Suhcrom, Suhcrom, come on. It's time for us to be nomads." Naddih shook his shoulder. "Wake up, Suhcrom. It's time to get up. Remember our plans?"

Suhcrom moaned as his head plopped back down onto the pillow.

Naddih cupped his hands around his mouth and crouched down close to Suhcrom's ear. "Cock-a-doodley-do! Cock-a-doodley-do!"

Suhcrom groaned louder. He reached up and put his hand over Naddih's mouth. "Stop pretending to be a stupid rooster."

"But is it working?" asked Naddih.

"No, it's not. You already woke me up makin' all that noise in the kitchen," Suhcrom laughingly grumbled. "What's that thing hanging around your head?"

Naddih giggled.

Suhcrom rubbed his eyes and took a good look at Naddih. "Why are you wearing your sunglasses...and water boots? And what's in that bag?"

"Some pots and plates, and cups, some plastic knives and spoons, and Mama's kettle. Stuff for our adventure."

"Have you gone mad? We don't need all that stuff." Suhcrom gestured to Naddih and turned his head away. "Now go away. Let me sleep a little bit longer."

"But you said we'd be nomads today, remember?"

"I know, but I'm tired. We can be nomads tomorrow," Suhcrom mumbled and flipped his pillow over his face.

"Please, Suhcrom," Naddih pleaded. "You promised."

Suhcrom rolled over on his back and yawned. He'd been excited about this adventure for days; but this morning he was just too tired. It was only five o'clock— way too early to wake up. However, he had promised

Naddih they would go right after their father left for work. His mind drifted back to the plans they had made several days earlier....

❮

They had been watching a documentary and it captivated their interest immediately. The nomads on TV spoke in Arabic, so Suhcrom and Naddih tried to keep up by reading the English subtitles. The narrator told the story with a stately British accent. They watched with intrigue as the nomads wandered on their camels across the vast desert somewhere in a faraway land. It was fascinating how these nomads endlessly migrated from one area of the desert to another. They continually searched for the next oasis or a place where they could pitch their tents to rest their sheep.

Oh, to have the freedom to roam like the nomads! The boys both desperately wanted that kind of freedom. After watching the program, they had stayed up most of the night planning their adventure. Imitating the narrator's British accent, Suhcrom had recounted the entire documentary nearly word for word, going over every detail. Occasionally, Naddih rambled off some gibberish pretending to be speaking Arabic and then expected

Suhcrom to interpret what he was saying. Eventually, sleep had overtaken them. When they awakened the next morning, they began talking about it again. They could hardly wait. This was one of the most exciting things they had ever thought of. They were going to be nomads!

They wanted to get a tent. They began to think and think. What would make a good tent for nomads? They looked at each other with widened eyes and instantly knew what the other was thinking.

"A cardboard box!" they both shouted out at the very same time.

They set out immediately to the nearby grocery store to search for the biggest cardboard box they could find. It wasn't going to be too difficult. They knew there was always a big heap of discarded boxes outside the building. When the boys got to the store, they quietly snuck around to the side and began to rummage through the pile.

"Naddih, look at this one. It's huge." The box Suhcrom pointed to was one of the biggest boxes they had ever seen. "This will work great as a tent."

"Holy Macaroni, Suhcrom. That's gigantic! That will make the best nomad tent."

*Shhhk-shhhk-shhhk-shhhk.* The boys looked up and

saw the store clerk sweeping the sidewalk. She had her eye on them, watching intently. She stopped sweeping and started asking them a lot of questions.

"Hey, what are you boys doing out there? What do you need a box for?"

Suhcrom thought the clerk was being way too nosy, so he ignored her. He wanted to just get the box and run. Unfortunately there were a number of other discarded boxes and bottles on top of it. And it was going to be a little tricky pulling it out from underneath all of the debris. Sure enough, when he grabbed it from the pile, everything came toppling down. One of the bottles tumbled onto a nearby tin garbage can and bounced against the lid. *Kabang!*

Naddih sheepishly looked up at the clerk. "Saaaw-wy, Miss Shopkeeper lady."

"Just where do you boys think you're going with that, anyway?"

Suhcrom and Naddih didn't want to seem suspicious; it was so hard trying to keep their faces straight as they held back their laughter. They didn't want to give their secret away! So Suhcrom responded with the first thing that came to his mind.

"Uh, we need it to collect some bottles and cans. That's all," he replied.

"Hmm." The clerk pursed her lips as she raised her hand to her hip. "Bottles and cans, huh?" She nodded, finished sweeping the sidewalk and then went back into the store.

The box the boys had found was so big it took both of them to carry it home. Quickly they ran, Suhcrom holding one end and Naddih the other, both struggling to keep it from slipping out of their hands. They carried it around to the back of their house and hid it behind one of the coconut trees where no one would see it, especially their father. It would be safe there until they were ready to go on their adventure....

❭

Suhcrom sluggishly sat up on the couch. He tossed the pillows aside.

"Yes, you're right, Naddih. I did promise. So today we'll be nomads. But take off the sunglasses and those water boots. You look like you're going to hunt wild pigs; and we're not going to play Indiana Jones flying over the Serengeti, either."

Naddih laughed as he quickly slipped off his boots. *Whoosh!* He rushed off to the bedroom like a rocket. Suhcrom wiped the sleepiness from his eyes. He was just slipping on his shorts and tee shirt when Naddih returned, dressed and ready to go.

*"Heeee! Heeee!"* Naddih galloped around and around in a circle, waving his arms up and down, nickering and shaking his head like his favorite horse, Thunderbird. "It's time to be nomads, Suhcrom," he said grinning ear to ear.

"Shh, man, shh. You'll wake Enomih," Suhcrom said as he raised his finger to his lips. "Come on. We need to get our tent."

"Yes, yes, we need our tent," Naddih echoed.

"And we have to get a few supplies," added Suhcrom.

"Yes, yes, I've got a few supplies," Naddih recited after Suhcrom.

"Why are you repeating everything I say, Naddih?" asked Suhcrom.

"Sorry, I can't help it. I'm just so excited!" Naddih squealed. He grabbed the sack of Mama's crockeries.

"Don't you touch that sack. I told you we don't need all that stuff. Now let's go."

So with their father gone until late that evening, and their sister still asleep in her room, the coast was clear. It was time for the boys to be on their way.

They tiptoed through the kitchen, filled a plastic liter soda bottle with water, and then scurried out of the house in their bare feet. They quickly grabbed their cardboard box from behind the coconut tree and quietly crept between the houses toward the street. Finally they were going to be nomads. It was all Naddih could do to keep from screaming out with excitement.

# CHAPTER 2

# Palmerston Close

Like two quiet little mice, these newly self-proclaimed nomads made it out of the house without waking their sister. It was their first stroke of luck. This wasn't easy considering all of the excitement and anticipation bottled up inside of them. A veil of darkness shielded them from view as they silently tiptoed through the concrete jungle of houses. But would they be able to get past the neighbors in Palmerston Close without being seen? That would be the next trick.

Palmerston Close was a small neighborhood within the town of Portsmouth on the island of Jamaica, West Indies. The town had been established as a residential development for a long time and was very family-oriented. Suhcrom, ten years old, and Naddih, eight, had moved there five years ago. They lived there along with their older sister, Enomih, who was thirteen, and their father, Evrohl, whom they affectionately called "Jomfeh."

It didn't take long for the boys to adapt to their new

home. It was like living with one big family the way all of the neighbors watched out for each other. It was common for one family to look after another family's children, taking them in for meals or keeping them overnight. This was the Jamaican way.

On most days, the boys saw their neighbors sitting outside of their houses, watching other people walk by. Usually they were just checking things out and wondering what was going on in the town. It was typical to hear their daily greetings of *"Howdy!"* or *"How yuh a do?"* Perhaps you would even hear them exclaim, *"It's an irie day, mi fren!"* as they called out to each other in their native language, Patois. Suhcrom and Naddih found their neighbors very friendly and Palmerston Close truly a nice place to live. Everyone seemed to know everyone else, and they all seemed to know each other's business. So the boys quickly realized that sneaking around without anyone finding out was nearly impossible!

The street Suhcrom and Naddih lived on was a dead-end, and formed a big square area in front of the houses that became the neighborhood playground. Many of the children gathered there because it made a great place to hang out with friends, kick a soccer ball around, play hopscotch, Dandy Shandy and other games. It wasn't unusual to have as many as thirty kids playing there at the same time, some from early afternoon until late into the evening.

With so many children their age to play with, Suhcrom and Naddih had quickly formed a close group of friends. Sterlin and his younger brother, Rodney, were their closest. They saw them nearly every day and did almost everything together. There was Amos, too. Then there were Mikal and Peter, and Mouse and Hamburg. Mouse's real name was Cordell, but nobody ever called him that. Kids called him "Mouse" because he had a small build and was very soft spoken. And, Hamburg? Well, no one was sure what his real name was. There was no Burger King or McDonald's around at the time so it was a mystery how he even got that name. Perhaps it was simply because he liked to eat beef patty and coco bread. Whatever the reason, it didn't really matter. To them he was just "Hamburg." They were a tight group of friends, a crazy bunch of kids!

"I wish we could have asked Sterlin and Rodney to be nomads with us," Naddih mumbled softly.

"I know," Suhcrom replied quietly. "But you know we couldn't tell them. We need to keep this a secret. They'll laugh at us. Besides, everybody thinks we're up to something whenever we're with those guys. Ha-ha, remember the time we went to the swamp to catch crabs...?

Now these boys knew they weren't allowed to be near the swamp alone, especially at night; but the four of them had been scheming for some time. And of course, they didn't want anyone to know what they were up to. So their plan was to meet at a secret location.

They made sure they had the necessary supplies—a *crocus bag* and an oil lamp. The crocus bag was made out of a heavy coarse burlap-type material and had a draw-string closure. These were very common in Jamaica and because they were so strong, they were used to carry just about anything. The boys had used one many times before when catching crabs. It worked the best for carrying home their catch.

The oil lamp had been crafted from an empty glass soda bottle with some kerosene poured into it. Then they had ripped up one of Suhcrom's old shirts and stuffed it into the kerosene to make the wick. It was crude, but it definitely worked for what they needed.

They set out a little after nine o'clock at night. Except for some moonlight, and what little firelight they had from the oil lamp, they were surrounded by total darkness. Naddih stayed close beside Suhcrom, tightly clutching his shirt. Barefoot, the four of them tromped through the thick blades of swamp grass and bamboo shoots. They tromped through the sticky mud near the edges of the swamp, and before they knew it, they were knee-deep in the black, tarry, murky waters that smelled of rotten fish.

About an hour into the search, they were ready to give up when Rodney spotted something moving in the dim moonlight.

*"Luk ova desso man, shine di light ova desso,"* Rodney whispered. *"Mi tink mi see a crab movin' ova desso."*

Naddih, who was carrying the lamp at the time, shined the light over in the direction where Rodney was pointing. There it was—the biggest, most gigantic crab they had ever laid eyes on.

"Holy Smackaroni! That thing is bigger than Sterlin's cat, Stanky Spanky." Naddih's jaw dropped in disbelief. He had never seen such an enormous crab.

As soon as the light exposed it, the crab stood still and the boys realized they had caught it smack dab in the middle of eating its dinner. They couldn't tell exactly what it was eating, but as they moved slowly forward, the telltale stench gave it away. It didn't take long to figure out that this humongous crab was deep into the belly of a big, old, smelly rotten mullet, and having the feast of its life! The crab spooked and ran off, and the four of them were in hot pursuit, chasing after their prey, screaming and laughing like a bunch of hyenas.

"Bring the bag over here, man!"

"No, wait...over there, over there."

"Quick, it's comin' out of the hole."

"Hurry, man, hurry!"

*Phluug, phluug, phluug, phluug*...their feet sunk into the sticky mud as they chased that crab through the murky brackish water. They chased it back and forth, in and out of holes, and straight into the crocus bag. There it was, trapped and stinking to high heaven!

They all felt pretty darn proud of pulling this off. When they got the crab back home, they let it loose in the street.

*"Ahhh! Ahhh!"* All of the kids screeched as the gigantic crab scurried frantically around.

*"Eeeeew,"* they cried out. "That stinks!"

Later the next day, after a thorough washing of course, the crab was boiled in a big pot with some salt and a healthy dose of scotch bonnet pepper. It was the best crab they'd ever eaten. Neither Jomfeh nor Benton, Sterlin and Rodney's father, had even thought to question where the crab came from, so no one was the wiser

to the boys' mischievous scheme and the events of the night before. Oh, the thrill of the hunt....

◗

As Suhcrom and Naddih made their way through the houses in the Close, they passed by Sterlin and Rodney's home. They paused and glanced at each other. Those boys were their best friends, but they hadn't said a single word to them about this exciting nomad adventure. Naddih had really wanted to tell them. After all, this was the most awesome idea they had ever come up with.

"Are you sure we can't say anything to them?" asked Naddih.

"Are you kidding me?" Suhcrom snickered. "Uh-uh, we can't tell those guys. Being nomads? They'll think we're crazy, man. They'll laugh their heads off."

*"Yah mon, like di time wi a go sell Tiki Tiki to dem fishermen?"* Naddih giggled.

"Yeh, they thought that was ridiculous...trying to sell baby mullet fish to people who catch fish for a living," Suhcrom chuckled.

"And...and, and then they went and told Hamburg and Amos," Naddih reminded Suhcrom.

"Yes, and you know what a big mouth Amos has," Suhcrom exclaimed.

Naddih agreed wholeheartedly. "Yes, Suhcrom, being nomads will be our special adventure. If we tell them, they will go and tell Hamburg and Amos again, and then the whole world is gonna hear about it. We'd be the laughing stock of all Palmerston Close!"

The boys glanced one last time at Sterlin and Rodney's house, and then quickly moved on. Their secret nomad adventure was about to begin.

# CHAPTER 3

# The Desert Awaits

**N**addih was just a bundle of nervous energy as they started down the sidewalk. He became fidgety. There was no way he could contain his excitement any longer.

"Suhcrom, Suhcrom, I can't wait until we can roam the desert!" he said in a loud whisper.

"Shh, Naddih, be quiet. Don't talk. We can't let the neighbors hear us. We have to get down to the end of the street past all of the houses without anyone seeing us. *Yah mon*, let's hurry."

In spite of the lingering early morning darkness, sneaking by the neighbors in Palmerston Close wasn't going to be easy. Suhcrom couldn't help but smile to himself though; he felt giddy because sneaking by all of the neighbors only added more mystery to their adventure!

"Come on, Naddih, we better hurry," Suhcrom said as he giggled quietly.

*"Mi a hurry Suhcrom, but di box a slip outta mi hands."*

They paused for just a moment to regain their hold

on the box and then set off again. Finally, they reached the end of the street at the edge of town. They had successfully navigated through the concrete jungle of houses without being noticed, possessively clutching the cardboard box that would be their nomad tent.

Soon the morning broke and the sun beat down on their closely shaven heads. The sky was clear, not even a single cloud, and it began to get hot. Beads of sweat formed across their foreheads. Before long, the sweat began to slowly trickle down along the sides of their faces, dripping down their necks, dampening the collars of their shirts.

"Man, it's hot out here already," Suhcrom exclaimed as he wiped his face with his shirt sleeve.

In true nomad style, the boys simultaneously peeled off their shirts and wrapped them like turbans around their heads.

"Ha-ha! Look at us, Naddih," Suhcrom said with glee. "We're *real* nomads now. We have our turbans on just like the nomads on TV!"

"Yes, Suhcrom. We're just like them—with our turbans *and* our tent. And soon we'll be roaming the desert in search of an oasis."

They came to the end of the street in Palmerston Close that led to a huge field. To the far left of the field was the swamp. It lay just inland from the ocean that bordered the back of their neighborhood. Suhcrom and Naddih knew it well, of course. They had explored there many times before with their friends. To the far right of the field, they could see construction still underway where several new buildings had taken shape along the horizon. This was the site of the new Hart Academy, an all-boys trade school.

The field itself was entirely surrounded by a tall chain link fence with the biggest, most massive gate ever created by mankind. Suhcrom and Naddih had no idea how high the gate was. But they guessed it must have stood at least fifty feet high and fifty feet wide. It was *huge!* And they were quite familiar with it. They had climbed it before with Sterlin and Rodney the day they were caught trespassing in the field, one of the times those four boys had gotten into mischief. Adrenaline pulsed through their veins as the memory of that day vividly came back.

"Suhcrom," Naddih said with a smirk on his face, "Remember when we were spotted in this field by that crazy old man on the bulldozer?"

"I remember it like it was yesterday, Naddih." Suhcrom shook his head and chuckled as a silly crooked grin slowly spread across his face....

❛

Naddih wanted to search for some boards that he could use to build himself a pigeon coop. So the boys set out with Sterlin and Rodney to explore around the town. When they got to the field, Naddih eyed a stack of plywood off in the distance, over near the area where work was being done on the Hart Academy. Naddih wanted that wood. And he was determined to have it!

The gate was closed—and for good reason. It was plain to see that a *LOT* of construction was going on. *Ddddd...dddd! Ddddd...dddd!* The sound of jackhammers and the *clang, clang, clang* of steel beams could be heard in the distance. A bright yellow sign was posted on the gate: "DANGER – CONSTRUCTION ZONE." It may as well have been an invitation. As these four rascals stood at the gate reading the sign, they accepted it as a challenge to get into more mischief! So they climbed the fence and started off towards the wood pile.

Not very far into their trek across the field they were spotted by one of the construction workers on his bulldozer. None of the boys had seen him. He came out of nowhere and the terrifying chase began. That crazy man headed right towards them on his massive machine at record speed. He was waving his hands and shouting things at the boys that made their ears curl! The boys started screaming and running every which way. Eventually, they all headed back towards the gate with that gigantic bulldozer bucket right on their heels.

Naddih, the fastest runner, and Sterlin, the best climber, reached the gate first and climbed for all they were worth. Both were up and over it in a flash. Suhcrom and Rodney were a little slower at climbing and lagged behind. Sterlin stood frozen as he stared from the other side of the gate. Naddih, in a panic, screamed at the top of his lungs.

"Climb, Suhcrom, climb! *HURRY!*"

Suhcrom and Rodney weren't even halfway up the fence when that crazy man raised his bucket to scoop them up. It was too scary to watch. Naddih felt sick to his stomach. Suhcrom and Rodney scurried just out of the bucket's reach and finally made it up over the gate. The four of them high-tailed it out of there, running as fast as they could, shaking their fists and screaming in terror.

*"A weh yu a do? Yu crazy, man, yu crazy! Yu waa fi kill wi?"*

The old man was wild with laughter as he watched the boys run away. They never forgot that frightening experience, but as time passed, they were able to laugh about it. And each time they recounted the story, the tale got taller—and more outrageous....

❧

*"Di man was so crazy.* I never saw a bulldozer move that fast, man. What if he'd caught us? Ha-ha, we were running for our lives that day, Suhcrom. For our *LIVES!"*

"Yes, you're right, Naddih. Ha-ha, you sure do have a way with words. I thought for sure we would die that day."

*"A gud ting Jomfeh no know 'bout it,"* Naddih exclaimed.

"Fear made me climb the gate that day, Naddih. It was fear pure and simple. If that crazy man on the bull-dozer didn't kill us, Jomfeh would have—if he'd known." Suhcrom shuddered at the memory.

Since that day, the boys had returned to this field many times without incident, but they never had to climb that enormous gate again. Mysteriously, a hole had been cut in the fence and they had been able to wander in and out without much notice.

So here they were, on the first day of their nomad adventure, finding themselves once again at the entrance of the field. It was a mass of sand, dirt, rocks, and a few random clumps of flowering weeds as far as the eye could see. Strangely, the huge gate had been left wide open today. With nothing between them and the field, they stood, motionless, staring out across this wide open space. This was their desert.

Suhcrom and Naddih stood still for several moments longer, and gazed intently. They cast aside all of their unpleasant memories of the bulldozer chase. And they weren't the least bit interested in chasing crabs in the swamp or looking at what was being built at the trade school. Not today. At this moment, they were focused on one thing and one thing only—being nomads. The anticipation bubbled up inside of them. Their minds raced with wild imagination. And Suhcrom's heart pounded so hard it felt like it would burst right out of his chest!

As the two of them walked through the open gate, they felt magically transported out of the field in Palmerston Close into some faraway land. The hot sun beat down on their heads while their vivid imaginations carried them right into the middle of the desert. They had so desperately longed for this! Naddih raised his hand to his forehead to shade his view. He gleamed with joy as he peered across the rippling mounds in front of him. Nothing but sand for miles! A soft breeze blew the tiny grains of sand into miniature cyclones across the dunes, looking just like the desert in the documentary.

With steady progression, the boys continued to drift along in awe of the amazing world they had just entered. They could almost hear the British narrator talk about this faraway land and the nomads who wandered for days in search of water.

*Baa-baa-baa.* Naddih turned his head. He paused to listen.

"Suhcrom, did you hear that? It sounds like sheep." He looked off in the distance and thought he caught a glimpse of something moving on the horizon. "Look, over there. Maybe it's some other nomads!"

"Huh? Oh, that's probably just Mr. Palmer walking his two goats, Lamb Chop and Rib Eye," Suhcrom chuckled.

"Noooo.... Why would Mr. Palmer be in our desert? I definitely see sheep, lots of sheep, not goats."

As Naddih glanced over at Suhcrom, he saw images of Mamadou, the little shepherd boy in the documentary, tending the sheep. He suddenly realized, at that very moment, that they had turned into the mystical nomads of their dreams; and they were about to embark on the most thrilling adventure of their lives...*EVER!*

# CHAPTER 4

# Freedom to Roam

"Oh, wow. Look at us, Suhcrom, we're real nomads. Ha-ha, we're finally real nomads," screamed Naddih.

Suhcrom grinned in awe.

"Can you believe it, Suhcrom? Now we can roam the desert forever," Naddih cried out as they both jumped up and down with joy.

In the far distance, towards the back corner of the field, they spotted an impressively tall hill of dirt. It raised high above the ground and its softly rounded peak pointed toward the sky with such dignity.

"Naddih, look at it. See it way out there?" Suhcrom pointed toward the hill. "Isn't it magnificent?"

Naddih's eyes grew wide with wonder. "Wow! That is one big hill, Suhcrom. I bet it's at least a mile high!"

"Ha-ha, maybe Naddih. That's our destination. That's where we'll set up our nomad tent. *Yah mon*, let's get going."

The nomads began to wander across their desert in a comfortable silence as the breeze swirled around their faces. Oh, the sweet taste of magical, mystical freedom! They had planned this for days and could hardly believe they were finally here. It was overwhelming. Never in their wildest dreams did they imagine it could be so amazing.

As they journeyed along, Naddih heard the voice of the British narrator recounting the remarkable things about the desert. It was a marvel to him that the desert got so hot during the day, but then so cold at night. The boys continued, absorbed in their own thoughts, enjoying their new identities. Before long, these nomads would reach the hill where they would pitch their tent and rest.

The silence was broken when Naddih unexpectedly called out to Suhcrom.

"*Chak'awaa bakayuh poolahseh,*" he proclaimed sternly.

Suhcrom burst out laughing. *"A weh yu a seh, man?"* He glanced at Naddih with a confused look. "What was *that* supposed to be?"

"I'm speaking Arabic like the nomads in the *doctamentry*. Tell me what I just said, Suhcrom," Naddih replied indignantly.

"That was no Arabic, Naddih. That was just silly gibberish. How am I supposed to know what you said?"

Suhcrom laughed again. "And by the way, it's documentary, not *doctamentry*."

"I said, 'We need to have a camel and some sheep.' That's how I say it in Arabic," Naddih replied, feeling just a little offended. "In the *doctamentry*, the nomads had camels to ride on and sheep to herd across the desert."

"You only said, like, three words, Naddih," Suhcrom teased. "*Chebelak nago head,* or whatever—that's supposed to mean all of that?"

"That's not what I said, Suhcrom. I said, '*Chak'awaa bakayuh poolahseh.*' That's how I say it in my Arabic," Naddih insisted.

"You're silly, Naddih. But if you're saying we need a camel and some sheep, then yes, I agree. We need some wives, too!" Suhcrom added jokingly.

"Wives? What do we need them for?" asked Naddih.

"Those nomads had wives to tend the sheep and cook the food," explained Suhcrom.

The boys continued to wander deep in thought when they were suddenly caught off guard by a huge gust of wind. Fiercely it whipped around them; it slapped at their faces and shrouded them in a dusty funnel of sand. It blew so hard it practically ripped their turbans right off of their heads! Then, without warning, the inevitable happened—the wind snatched their prized cardboard tent from their grip and sent it flipping about in a jagged path across the desert.

"Catch it, Suhcrom. Quick, before it blows away!" Naddih cried out. With all of the sand and dirt blowing in his eyes, Naddih could barely see which way to run.

Suhcrom chased after the tent as fast as he could. He ran first to the left, and then to the right, whichever way the wind blew.

"I've got it—*Blast!*" Suhcrom almost had it, and then away it blew. Again he scrambled after it. It looked like a wild goose chase as he ran this way, then that way. "I have...wait...I've...aha...I've got it!" Just as Suhcrom reached out to grab it, another gust of wind tossed it around. It danced in another direction, just out of his reach. *"Daaang...."*

Naddih, still in the chase, tugged frantically on his pants to keep them from falling down. He was wearing shorts handed down to him from Suhcrom, twice his size and very baggy. He loved these shorts, but he never wore them with a belt. So these supersized pants were quickly slipping down over his lanky frame. They wrapped and twisted around his legs, nearly tripping him; he struggled just to stay standing. He darted back and forth in every direction, trying to catch the box with one hand while holding his shorts up with the other. He wasn't getting anywhere too quickly!

"Suhcrom, Suhcrom, wait. I can't run," Naddih screamed. He laughed as he staggered to the left, almost toppling over. "My shorts are falling off. Suhcrom, wait."

"What? Come on Naddih. We've got to catch it before we lose it," Suhcrom shouted back.

Stumbling along, Naddih ran in the opposite direction of Suhcrom. He figured he could grab the box if his brother couldn't. He was bound and determined to get it, and he didn't want to be embarrassed by losing his pants in the process.

So, with their turbans flopping and Naddih's shorts twisted at his knees, these young nomads ran in circles, giggling childishly as they chased after the cardboard box. The chase made them dizzy with laughter! Finally, the wind settled down long enough for Suhcrom to grab hold of it. Naddih tripped over toward Suhcrom, and they both collapsed into a heap on top of the box. They felt silly and very out of breath.

"Oh man, Naddih," Suhcrom gasped. "That was so funny." He couldn't control his laughter as he rolled around in the dirt. "And you...you with...you with your shorts falling down, man!"

*"Yah mon, mi pants...mi pants a drop off...."* Naddih burst into hysterical laughter. He knew how ridiculous he must have looked. Their amusement grew wild as they thought about it all over again.

"Oh my goodness, Suhcrom, I didn't think we were *ever* going to catch that thing." Naddih hugged his ribs. They ached so badly from all the laughter and from the intensity of the chase as well.

*"Eeeeeh,"* Suhcrom gasped for air. "I've got to catch my breath, Naddih. *Eeeeeh,* my asthma is coming on."

Suhcrom had experienced a few bouts with asthma as a young child, but he had long since outgrown it. In fact, he hadn't had an attack in years. Still, he always feared its return. He carried his old inhaler in his pocket just in case, but he never really did learn how to use it correctly. The mouthpiece was scratched and rather dirty, and he wrinkled his nose up as he looked at it with a bit of humorous disgust. Then, holding the inhaler about six inches away from his mouth, he pretended to suck in a couple of quick little puffs.

"Let me have some puffs, Suhcrom. I think my asthma is coming on, too!" Naddih gasped.

"Naddih, you don't have asthma," Suhcrom said, still short of breath.

"I think it might be starting right now." Naddih

burst out laughing again as he fell backwards. "Hey, Suhcrom, what if we hadn't caught our tent? We couldn't be nomads without our tent."

Naddih sprawled out on his back, still trying to catch his breath. "I would have been one sorry nomad with no tent—and no pants either!" His chest heaved and he tried to swallow, but all of the chasing and running around had made him really thirsty.

"Suhcrom, Suhcrom quick, where is our water bottle? My throat is so dry. My tongue is sticking to the roof of my mouth." Naddih adjusted his shorts and sat up on his knees. He panted as he reached out his hand to beg for a drink.

Suhcrom dragged himself up off the ground and searched around to find where they had dropped the water bottle. "I know it was right around here some-where...oh, here it is, Naddih. I found it." Suhcrom grabbed the bottle and returned to see Naddih waving his hand in urgency.

"Hurry, I'm so thirsty. I can barely swallow," Naddih said as he reached out for the water.

"Hold on, hold on. I need some too, you know," said Suhcrom. He hesitated before handing the water to Naddih. "We can only have one sip each."

"What? One sip? Is that all?" Naddih groaned.

"We only brought one bottle, Naddih. Remember how the nomads had to ration their supplies?" reminded Suhcrom. "This has to last us all day."

"Yes, yes, yes, of course I remember, Suhcrom. Now please, let me have a sip. *Please*...I'm so thirsty."

They each took a swig. It was clear that wasn't enough, so they each took another. *Swish-swish-swish-swish.* Both of the boys puffed out their cheeks and swirled the water around in their mouths.

Naddih tipped his head back and stroked the front of his throat. *Girrrrgle...girrrrgle.* He giggled at the sound. *Girrrrgle...girrrrgle. Gulp. GULP!* He began to gag and choke on the water. The next thing he knew the water had spewed out of his mouth *and* his nose—and all over Suhcrom. He raised his eyebrows sheepishly.

*"A weh yu do dat fa, man?"* Suhcrom shook his head as he wiped the water off his chest. "You're wasting the water, Naddih. Come on, I think we've had enough for now."

So with their thirst adequately quenched for the moment, the boys rewound their turbans, secured their holds on the cardboard tent, and continued to wander across the last part of their desert. The hill was their destination.

# CHAPTER 5

# To the Hill

Neither Suhcrom nor Naddih had watches on, but judging by the position of the sun, and how long they had been walking, Suhcrom figured it was mid-morning, maybe about ten o'clock. They had recuperated from the tent chase and their excitement about reaching the hill was building. Just as their pace hastened, Naddih happened to notice something peculiar on the ground ahead.

"Suhcrom, look over there. Look, what is that?" Naddih ran over to where he saw a strange pile of bones lying in a clump of weeds. He turned back and called out again to Suhcrom.

"Suhcrom, come here. Look at this. Bones. A skeleton, Suhcrom." Naddih shuddered as he urgently waved for Suhcrom to come and see. "Some poor nomad died out here wandering across the desert. *Poor ting*. He probably died from thirst. Or maybe from sun stroke... or a snake bite. Maybe he was eaten by a wild animal or something. I wonder if his family misses him. Boy, I sure hope that doesn't happen to us." Naddih's lip quivered.

Suhcrom ran over to where Naddih was standing. This was one of the most unusual things they had ever come across.

"*Man, a wa dat?*" Suhcrom asked curiously. He picked up a stick and poked at the bones. *Crrrrk.* They were so dry and brittle they crumbled under the slightest touch. *Crrrrk, crrrrk.* Naddih gasped; he never saw bones break and turn to dust before. It was really weird—and spooky.

"Whoa, do you see that?" Suhcrom jumped back and let out a nervous laugh. He stepped closer again and kicked at the bones with his bare foot until several of them had pulverized.

"Suhcrom, don't do that," Naddih pleaded. "Stop... you'll get gangrene in your toes."

"Gangrene? That's nonsense, Naddih. It won't hurt anything," Suhcrom chuckled. He gave the bones another strike. "I'd have to have an open cut on my toe... and then be bitten by a stinkin' mosquito for me to ever get gangrene."

Naddih considered this for a moment. This didn't sound right to him. "You get *malalaria* from *mozziquitoes*, Suhcrom, not gangrene."

Suhcrom smiled. "*Malalaria* Naddih? What is *malalaria*? Don't you mean malaria?"

"But am I right or not, Suhcrom? I heard Jomfeh say you get malaria from mosquitoes. And Mama said the same thing, too."

*"Mi no know 'bout dat, man,"* Suhcrom said. He shrugged his shoulders as he let out a big huff. He had been trying to mess with Naddih's mind, but realized it had kind of backfired on him.

"So who do you think this could be, Suhcrom?" Naddih asked.

"How would I know? Pretty hard to tell, don't you think? Could be a human, could be an animal maybe," Suhcrom said. He inspected what was left of the dried broken ribcage. "Maybe it's Helmet. Remember Helmet?"

"Helmet?" Naddih looked puzzled. "Helmet's a game, Suhcrom."

"Yeh, I know it's a game we play. But all the old people say it was named after Helmet, that blind dog people always talked about. You know, the one they think got snatched by a giant swamp creature."

Suhcrom began to tell Naddih the story he'd heard about the legendary dog named Helmet. Everyone said it was a mystery how this dog strangely vanished into thin air. It happened many, many years ago, long before they had moved to Palmerston Close. Folklore passed down through the ages told of how Helmet had suddenly appeared in the town one day. No one knew where he had come from or to whom he belonged.

"What I heard was that some of the town squatters took him in...fed him and took care of him for a while," said Suhcrom.

"Fed him what?" Naddih cast a curious look at Suhcrom.

"Who cares what they fed him. Maybe it was *festival* and sprat fish," Suhcrom teased. "Whatever it was, it didn't help his eyesight any."

"What do you mean, Suhcrom?"

"He was blind. Nobody knew it, but the way I heard it, everybody in the village saw him walking into things, like trees and lampposts. He'd even walk into kids, too!"

"Wait, so he walked into things? Like, if he was going along and, *BANG!* His head hits a tree. Or, or, *BAM!* He runs into a lamppost. Didn't that hurt his head or something?"

"I guess not. People say it never fazed him. Don't you see, Naddih? That's how he got his name. It was like his head was protected by a helmet."

"Oh, I see," Naddih nodded his head. "So whatever happened to him?"

"Well, the story was that Helmet liked to wander, and it wasn't unusual for him to leave for days on end.

But one day, he wandered off and never came back. He just mysteriously disappeared...the same way he came."

"That's it. He just left?"

"*Noooo*. Ask around sometime. You'll hear different versions of the story. People think there is a *lot* more to it. Most townspeople believe that a giant swamp monster captured him while he was wandering through the marshes." Suhcrom clawed his hands and hissed through his teeth. "*Roarrrrr!*"

"Ooooh," Naddih shivered at the horrible thought. "Poor Helmet."

"Yeh, but everybody loved him. He was such a beloved dog that people wanted to honor his memory after he disappeared. So, as a way to keep his memory alive, they made up a game for kids to play."

"Oh, I get it now Suhcrom. Helmet was blind. So in the game, that's why we have to walk around blindfolded." Naddih grinned. Finally it was making a little more sense to him.

"Yes, but they played it a little different back then. It started out where they blindfolded the kids and spun them around and around 'til they were so dizzy, man. Then they stood back and made fun while the kids stumbled into trees and stuff."

"*Yah mon*, like that time we were playing with Sterlin, remember? Man, we twirled him around and around and around, and, *WHAM!* He fell on his butt and we all started laughing, ha-ha-ha!"

"Yeh, that was funny. Anyway, now we play the game differently. Now we have the maze. Somewhere along the way we threw in a little bit 'o dis and a little bit 'o dat, stacked up a few juice boxes, and stones and shoes; and before you knew it, we had this awesome maze that you have to walk through blindfolded. We Jamaicans are *very* resourceful when it comes to games," Suhcrom said proudly.

"Okay, so whose bright idea was it to put soldiers in there?" asked Naddih.

"Soldiers? What are you talking about, Naddih?"

"The soldiers—you know, the kids who stand outside the maze and hit you on the feet if you step outside the maze. *WHACK!* Ouwee, it stings. That part is no fun, Suhcrom. It hurts."

"How would I know? I didn't make up the rules, Naddih. It must've been some crazy Jamaican who came up with that idea." Suhcrom chuckled. "Sounds like you've wandered outside the maze a few times *buoy*."

"Yeh, a few," admitted Naddih. "It's fun, but kinda scary. All those kids are blindfolded and trying to get through the maze at the same time. You don't know where you're going, or if you're inside or out. Then you get knocked out of bounds, and you get your feet whacked... and no one wants to be last, Suhcrom. *No one.* You know you're in trouble when you hear the word, 'HELMET.' Then everybody is chanting that stupid song, '*Crash-crash, Bang-bang, Helmet's finished last again! Crash-crash, Bang-bang, Helmet's finished last again!*'"

"Yeh, I don't like that song. Because whenever you hear it, it means you have to go back through the maze all over again!"

*"Yah mon, mi no waa fi be last. Cuz mi poor little feet cyaa tek di switches, man."* Naddih shook his head back and forth.

"I guess you're not too good at playing that game, huh?" Suhcrom laughed.

The boys turned their focus back to the bones on the ground.

"Suhcrom, do you really think these could be Helmet's bones?" Naddih asked quietly.

"It could be, Naddih," Suhcrom replied.

"Should we bury them? I wouldn't want anybody to step on them and get a horrible infection or something," Naddih said with concern.

*"Mi no tink nobody will get an infection, man. But*

*we can bury di bones. Mi no waa any of dem wild dogs eatin' di bones and disrespectin' mi fren, Helmet!"*

The boys kicked up the sandy dirt with their bare feet to cover the bones the best they could. Then they broke off a few stems of the nearby weeds and laid them reverently on top of the heap.

Suhcrom bowed his head and folded his hands in prayer. "Buddha bless Helmet," he said quietly. There was silence. He glanced to the side. Naddih stood quietly with his head bowed and eyes closed. Suhcrom nudged him with his elbow and gave him a curt nod.

"Huh?" Naddih opened his eyes. "Oh, Buddha bless you," he whispered, echoing Suhcrom's blessing. He leaned down, scooped up a handful of dirt and sprinkled it over the grave.

"Ashes to ashes. Dust to dust," Naddih said prayerfully.

*P-f-f-f-f-f-f-f-f!* Suhcrom tried to stifle his laughter.

"What's so funny?" Naddih wondered.

"That's not part of what the monks said in *Shaolin Temple Master.*"

"Well, those monks don't know everything, Suhcrom. They're not *uniscience.*"

"The word is omniscient, Naddih. Omniscient."

"That's what I said, Suhcrom. 'Uniscience.' They don't know it all."

"Okay, okay, you're right, Mr. Smarty-pants. *Yah mon*, we need to get going if we're going to make it to that hill sometime today."

Having made a meager attempt at giving a decent burial to what may have been Helmet, Suhcrom and Naddih finally put this interesting distraction behind them and got back on track to make their way to the hill. As they meandered across the desert, they slid back into their nomad identities with their moods merry once again. It wasn't long before they reached their destination.

"Finally we're here, Naddih." Suhcrom looked up to the top of the hill. "All we have to do is climb up there, pitch our tent, and then spend the rest of the day looking out over the whole desert. We'll be able to see everything from up there."

They stood at the base of the most gigantic pile of dirt they had ever seen. Now to some, the hill may not have looked terribly daunting. But to these two young nomads, who only stood about four feet high themselves, it looked to be a beast of a hill.

So, with all of the determination they could muster, they focused their eyes on the peak.

Suhcrom raised his hand high to lead the charge, and with his best imitation of the TV narrator's British accent, he gave the order.

"To the bloody hill!" he shouted.

With a mad rush, they both dug their heels into the gritty dirt and started climbing. Getting themselves up the hill was one thing. Carrying a huge cardboard box with the wind gusting around them was another.

*"Di wind a blow dirt in mi face,"* complained Naddih.

*"Wa?"*

*"Mi seh, di wind a blow dirt in mi face,"* Naddih shouted as loud as he could.

*"Mi cyaa hear weh yu a seh, man,"* Suhcrom yelled back.

*"Agh, mi no seh nuttin' man,"* Naddih mumbled under his breath. He spit out the gritty dirt from his mouth.

"Naddih, pick up the box, hold it up higher. It's slipping." Suhcrom was in the lead with Naddih struggling behind. They had made good progress and were almost to the top.

"Suhcrom, slow down, my shorts are falling off again. Slow down!"

"What?" Suhcrom yelled over his shoulder. He looked back at Naddih.

"My shorts are falling down," Naddih giggled. "Slow down, I can't climb that fast."

"We're nearly there, Naddih. Keep up with me. Just a couple more feet and we'll be there," Suhcrom said with encouragement. "Come on man, you can do it. Just pull up your pants and climb. And hold up the box!"

"I'm trying, Suhcrom. I'm trying...*Ahhhhhhh... Suhcrom...Ha-ha-ha-ha!*"

Naddih's legs buckled. Then he lost his footing. His arms gave out and he swiftly slid down the slope, laughing hysterically the whole way. Suhcrom, jerked backwards by Naddih's fall, slipped and lost hold of the box. But Naddih never let go of it. He hung onto that box for dear life.

As Suhcrom turned himself around, he saw Naddih flat on his stomach, his face covered with grit. His one hand dug deeply into the dirt; his other tightly clutched the cardboard box. And his baggy shorts? Well, instead of falling down, they were now scrunched up around his armpits.

They both laughed so hard that neither one of them could move. Naddih hoped Suhcrom could rescue him before his laughter made him too weak to hold on. Desperate, he struggled to keep from falling further down the hill. He burrowed his toes deeper into the dirt. And there was no way he would let go of that cardboard box.

"Suhcrom," Naddih begged. "Help me up. Hurry, help me up. Suhcrom, hurry...."

"Okay Naddih, I'm coming. Quick, grab onto my arm. I'll pull you up. And hang onto the tent. Don't let go for anything!"

Suhcrom reached down to pull Naddih up. He grasped Naddih's arm and hooked a couple of fingers through his belt loops. *HUUUUMPH!* With a swift upward thrust, Suhcrom heaved Naddih up to the top of the hill, tent in tow. As Naddih's feet plowed up through the dirt, it struck him how wonderful the cool dirt felt on his scorched feet. What a bizarre thought to have at such a moment.

Laughing and out of breath, they flopped down next to each other, amazed to have finally made it to the top of the hill. But they didn't want to waste any time. They quickly gathered themselves up and prepared to pitch their tent. Unfortunately, the cardboard box had gotten somewhat beaten and battered during all of the chaos.

"Oh, look at this Suhcrom, the corners are all torn." Naddih's shoulders slumped.

*"No, man. No worry 'bout it."* Suhcrom patted Naddih's shoulder. "It's okay. It's just bent up a little bit. It won't matter. It will still make a great tent."

They opened the box and folded the ends under to make it into a tunnel. Then they both crawled inside. It did make a fine tent indeed. Mission accomplished!

They lay there staring out across the desert. From the top of the hill, the view of the desert was even more striking than they had pictured. Suhcrom and Naddih gasped! They were nomads now. They had made it across the desert and to the top of the hill. Never in their wildest dreams did they imagine they would be here, resting in the shelter of their cardboard tent, in the most majestic spot in the whole wide world.

# CHAPTER 6

# Camels – Binoculars – Knives

It was early afternoon but their tent shielded them from the blistering midday sun. The grit of sand and dirt scratched against their legs; they were tired, hot, and thirsty, to say the least. Yet here they were, relaxing in the glorious view of their desert. As they lay there, Naddih's mind raced with thoughts about the documentary. He thought again of all the things the nomads had, such as camels, sheep, a dog to guard the sheep, and pots and pans to cook in. They even had binoculars. And knives, too.

"Suhcrom," Naddih said softly.

"Yea," Suhcrom mumbled. His eyes drooped as he began to drift off to sleep.

"Suhcrom," Naddih said again.

"Yes." Suhcrom popped an eye open.

"*Suhcrom!*" Naddih screamed.

"Yes Naddih, what *IS* it?" Suhcrom yelled.

"We need a camel."

Suhcrom curled up his lip and stared at Naddih. "A what?"

"A camel. *Hee-haw, hee-haw, brrrrrrr!*"

"Man, that's a donkey, not a camel," Suhcrom joked. "And don't spit on me."

"In the *doctamentry* those nomads had camels to ride across the desert."

"Just where do you think we're going to get a camel?" asked Suhcrom. "And I told you before, Naddih, its documentary, not *doctamentry*."

"We could make one," exclaimed Naddih.

"*A weh yu a seh, man?*" Suhcrom burst into laughter. "*Weh yu waa wi fi do?*"

He threw his head back and rolled around hysterically. He reached over and gave Naddih a teasing shove on the arm. "You are one silly nomad, Naddih. What do you think we're going to do, make one out of a cardboard box?"

"In the *doctamentry* those nomads had camels," Naddih replied sternly. He puckered his lips and frowned at Suhcrom. He wasn't pleased at all with Suhcrom's condescending tone. For him, the documentary was his guide, the Holy Grail, by which he would gauge whether or not they were true nomads. And *true* nomads had camels. But since he had no idea how they could make one, he decided he would move on to other things.

"Okay, Suhcrom, so what about binoculars? And what about a knife?"

Suhcrom thought for a moment. "Yes, we could definitely use some binoculars. Good idea, Naddih."

"Yeh, and...and...and we can use the binoculars to help us find the next oasis, too!" Naddih's face lit up, his excitement quickly returning as he saw Suhcrom's reaction to this idea. He dragged his finger through the dirt, drew a circle, and then marked an "X" in the middle. "Look, Suhcrom, we're here," he said, pointing to the "X." "The next oasis could be right over there. All we have to do is use our binoculars to find it. So where are we going to get binoculars, Suhcrom?"

Suhcrom paused to give it some more thought. "Ha! I know. We could make some!"

"Make some? Wait a minute; you thought it was crazy to make a camel. Now you want to make binoculars?" Naddih teased. "Just how do you think we're going to do that?"

"What if we took a couple of empty toilet paper rolls? We could glue them together with, hmm...maybe a matchbox. And maybe we could cover the ends with some plastic wrap—you know, to make it look like lenses. What do you think? We could do that, right Naddih? We'd have an amazing pair of binoculars."

"That's a great idea, Suhcrom. You're smart!" Naddih shouted. "Now, what about a knife? We need a knife, too."

A mischievous grin slowly spread across Suhcrom's face. A glint shone in his eyes. Naddih could tell Suhcrom was thinking of something really good in that crazy brain of his.

"I have an idea." Suhcrom leaned in closer to Naddih and whispered quietly. "We could use Jomfeh's knife. You know which one I'm thinking of? It looks exactly like the one Sylvester Stallone used in the movie *Rambo*."

"Oh no, no way, man. Uh-uh. I want a nomad knife more than anything; but I don't think that's such a good idea," Naddih said hesitantly. "You know what Jomfeh said to us, Suhcrom."

*"Mi know, mi know,* Naddih, but he'll never know. I swear."

"Are you sure? Because I don't want a whippin' on account of disobeying Jomfeh. Uh-uh, no way. I don't want another whippin' from Jomfeh ever again. It hurts. It hurts really bad!"

Suhcrom chuckled and brushed off Naddih's fears. "Don't be so silly, man. Leave it to me. I can get the knife. It's just until we can get our own anyway."

Suhcrom's words did little to reassure Naddih. He always looked up to Suhcrom and trusted whatever he said, but this time he wasn't buying it. He thought back to an incident that happened just a week ago this very day.

"I don't know, Suhcrom." Naddih shook his head and trembled. "What about when we went to the ocean by ourselves to catch crab? We got whipped hard for that... or have you forgotten?"

"No man, I remember," Suhcrom admitted. Their father had warned them repeatedly never to go to the ocean alone. Yet they had disobeyed.

"We'll get into trouble just like we did before, Suhcrom." Naddih recalled how horrible it was that day. Jomfeh had explained why he disciplined them so harshly, and he told them how sorry he was to have to do it. Still, the stinging pain of the whipping remained fresh in Naddih's mind even now.

Just then, a blustery gust of wind blew across the top of the hill. It swirled the dirt around like a tornado, swept through their tent, and puffed it up like a hot air balloon. In fact, the wind picked the tent up so high that the flap on Naddih's side pulled out from underneath him. Naddih, being so skinny, didn't weigh nearly enough to hold it down against the strength of the wind, and he wasn't quick enough to catch it. There was really no way to stop it. Over it flipped.

"Oh no, Suhcrom, not again," Naddih cried out. "We're going to lose our tent. Hold it down. Don't let it blow away!"

*"Mi a try, mi a try. Mi a do mi bes, man,"* Suhcrom shouted as he held on tightly.

Fortunately, Suhcrom weighed enough to hold his end secure and prevent the tent from sailing off down the hill. They could thank their lucky nomad stars for that. After several tries, Naddih finally grabbed hold of the loose flap. He quickly crawled back into the tent to keep it in place. As the wind died back down, the nomads settled back into their comfortable spots. They smiled and patted each other on the back, grateful that their tent was once again secure.

"You know, Suhcrom, I keep thinking about those nomads in the *doctamentry*. They had sheep, and a dog to guard the sheep. That's what we need." Naddih's mind turned and turned. "Where can we get some sheep?"

"In our heads, Naddih. They will exist in our imaginations. Or maybe we could borrow Lamb Chop and Rib Eye!"

Naddih giggled. *"Man, yu makin' mi hungry. Wi hav ani sandwiches?"*

"Oh no, are you kidding me? Naddih, we didn't bring anything to eat. What were we thinking?"

"We don't have anything to eat? Nuttin'? Not even a piece of bread?"

"Nuttin' man."

"Why didn't you bring any food, Suhcrom?"

"Me? You're the one who's always hungry. Why didn't you pack some food instead of all those useless pots and pans?"

"Cuz, I thought you'd get the food. You're the oldest. That's your job," Naddih said.

They talked on and on about how hungry they were as they rolled around in their merriment. How could they have forgotten food? They had spent days planning for this adventure, yet were so unprepared. They traveled across their desert with their tent and a full bottle of water, but they had no camel, no sheep, no binoculars, and no knife. And to top it off, they had no food. Silly Nomads!

"We will just have to tough it out, Naddih. What kind of nomads are we if we can't manage without food for a while?" Suhcrom reasoned.

"Camels can go a long time without food and water," Naddih interjected. "We are like the camels, Suhcrom."

"*Tek a gud look pon mi back, man. Yu see a hump?*" Suhcrom joked as he turned his back toward Naddih. "I don't know about you, but I'm no camel. I need some water. Pass me that water bottle."

They each took a few sips of water to wet their parched lips. Then they continued to talk about all of their crazy nomad dreams. Time passed quickly. Before they knew it, the afternoon had turned into early evening.

As dusk approached, Naddih gazed out over the desert. "Hey Suhcrom, look. *Mi see peenywallies.* Look, Suhcrom, lightning bugs! The *peenywallies* have come to light up our desert."

Suhcrom smiled as he watched the little lights flash on and off.

"Dem lightening bugs move like music notes, man. Look..." Naddih said.

"What?"

"Music notes. You know, like di orchestra...like dat famous composer, uh...uh...*Beeee–tovan,* ha-ha." Naddih raised his finger and swayed his hand in the air to the beat of the blinking lights. "Just like di orchestra."

"It's Beethoven...*Baay-to-ven,*" Suhcrom corrected.

"Yeh, whatever," Naddih giggled. Watching the peenywallies just tickled him.

And with one last burst of laughter, along with a few deep sighs, these two tired nomads gave in to their hunger and fatigue. Soon, they drifted quietly off to sleep at the end of this hazy, hot summer day, on the hill in the middle of their desert.

********

Suhcrom startled out of a sound sleep. He heard the crickets chirping and wondered just how long they had been sleeping. He looked out over the desert, and in the distance, he could see the rows of street lights in Palmerston Close. Suddenly, it struck him like lightning—they needed to get home...*now!*

"Naddih, Naddih, wake up, wake up," Suhcrom shouted. He vigorously shook Naddih's arm. "Wake up, man."

"What Suhcrom, what is it? Do you see other nomads?" Naddih rubbed the sleepiness out of his eyes, leaned up on his elbows and curiously peered out from under the tent.

*"Man, stop yu nonsense. Mi no see any ting like dat,"* Suhcrom scoffed. "But I do see us getting a whippin' if we don't take our tent down right now and get home. It's late. Jomfeh will be home from work soon. Hurry, we have to be home before he gets there!"

That's all Naddih needed to hear. He jumped up with a jolt before Suhcrom could blink his eyes.

*"Yah mon,* that's all we need...one of Jomfeh's *interrobations.* That wouldn't be good. That wouldn't be good at all." Naddih groaned as he shook his head.

"You mean interrogations, Naddih," said Suhcrom. "And yes, if we're not home when Jomfeh gets there, it won't be pleasant. We've got to keep our nomad adventure a secret."

"Suhcrom, can we come back tomorrow?" Naddih asked.

"Yes, yes, of course we can. We'll come with our binoculars and knife. Ha-ha, and maybe a camel and some sheep, too!" Suhcrom teased as he nudged Naddih with his elbow. "Now, let's grab our tent. We can't leave it here. We don't want any other nomads to steal it. *Yah mon*, we need to hurry."

The nomads gathered their cardboard tent and started down the dirt hill as fast as their legs could move. They ran so quickly they practically skid on air most of the way down, leaving a cloud of dust in their wake. Then with a few giant lunges, and a couple big jumps, they reached the bottom of the hill in no time flat. They were off and running!

"*Weeee!* Going down was a lot quicker than going up," Naddih squealed.

There was no time to waste, not one minute. With haste, the boys made it across the field, through the gate, and headed up the street towards home. As they passed the houses, the street lamps cast a beam of hazy light around them. Naddih shifted his eyes and caught a glimpse of Mouse's mother sitting on her front veranda with some of the neighbors. She was looking right at them. He quickly glanced away, but he could still feel her eyes following them as they shuffled up the street

The boys were a sight to behold. Exhausted, hot and covered with sand, they had no idea just how filthy they both looked. They had used their last bit of water to wash off the dirt, but it didn't help. They were still a mess from head to toe. They knew they looked rather obvious. Of course, carrying a big cardboard box made them even more conspicuous.

*"Hey, weh yuh boys been? Why yuh two so dutty?"* one of the neighbors called out.

Suhcrom and Naddih didn't say a word. They just looked straight ahead and kept on walking.

*"Hey, wah kinda mischievous tings yuh boys been up to?"* said Mouse's mother. *"Mi a go tell yuh faada!"*

They scurried on home as fast as they could, ignoring all of the comments. As they entered their yard, Suhcrom and Naddih both prayed silently that they had made it home before Jomfeh, and that no one would say a word about this to their father.

# CHAPTER 7

# The Nomads' Secret

The nomads hurried into their back yard, hid the tent behind the coconut tree, and silently crept into the house. Just as they entered the kitchen, they were stopped abruptly by their sister, Enomih.

Naddih's jaw dropped. "Uh-oh," he murmured under his breath. He gulped.

Suhcrom just stood there. He didn't dare speak.

*"A weh unu been all day?"* Enomih sputtered. *"Unu gone all day and left mi wid all di work."*

"But we...we..." Naddih started to explain.

*"Shush. Mi no waa fi hear no excuses. Di least unu can do is tek out di garbage. Mi hav to do every ting. Unu do nuttin'. Mi no know where yu been, and unu so dutty! Go bathe before wi eat."*

Fortunately, their father wasn't home from work yet. That was a stroke of luck. It was bad enough to get caught by Enomih. They ran off, quickly washed, and put on clean clothes; no one would have a clue these two mischievous boys were really nomads in disguise.

There were many things to do to prepare for their return journey the next day. Before their father got home, they needed to make the binoculars. They seized the moment.

"We need two of those cardboard toilet paper rolls, Naddih," said Suhcrom as he went into the bathroom. "There's got to be one here somewhere."

He knew his father had just put out a new roll of paper, so the empty one had to be in the waste basket. Suhcrom fished around in the garbage. He wrinkled his nose as he sifted through a pile of snotty tissues, egg shells, and banana peels.

"Eeeeew, this is gross! What's a half-eaten banana doing in here?"

"Oh, ha-ha," Naddih chuckled. "I took one of Enomih's bananas. I hid it in here 'til I could eat it. But she came after me, man. I only got half of it eaten before she came bangin' on the door."

"Of all the places you could go to eat, you picked the bathroom? You know what people do in here, right?"

Naddih shrugged his shoulders. He didn't care. It had been a good hiding place.

"I hate pawing through garbage!" Suhcrom grumbled. "Aha, I found it!" He smiled as he held up the prize. A string of banana peel hung limply on the edge of the roll.

"That's one down," Naddih exclaimed. Deciding he'd join in the hunt, he tipped the basket upside down and dumped its entire contents all over the bathroom floor.

"What are you doing, man?" Suhcrom shrieked.

"Well, we need two. So I'm looking for another one. We use a lot of toilet paper in this house. *Deh mus be one more roll in ya.*"

"I already went through the whole thing, Naddih. There isn't another one in there," replied Suhcrom. "Believe me. Now pick up that nasty banana peel because I'm *NOT* touching that."

"So, what now?" Naddih cocked his head. He hooked his thumb through his belt loop and gave his pants a tug.

"Look at you, man. Don't you have a belt? I'm gonna get you one for your birthday so your pants stop falling off," Suhcrom chuckled.

"*Mi pants fine, man. Nuttin' wrong wid it.* Come on, where we gonna find another roll?"

Suhcrom smirked. His head nodded in the direction of the brand new roll hanging on the holder. Before Naddih could blink an eye, Suhcrom had unraveled half of the roll. He continnued to spin it 'round and 'round until the whole roll was empty. They both peered into the toilet. There was a big heap of paper in there. A *huge* pile.

"*Suhcrom, dis no feel right, man.*" Naddih stared in disbelief. "Are we going to get in trouble for this?"

"No, not if you don't open your big mouth," Suhcrom cautioned. "*Yu a go keep yuh moute shut, right?*"

"Okay, I promise. I won't say anything, Suhcrom. I won't say anything even if they *interrobate* me!"

"*Interrobate?*" Suhcrom laughed. "I told you before, it's interrogate, not *interrobate,* Naddih. No one is going to interrogate you for wasting toilet paper you silly boy!"

Naddih wasn't so sure about this even though Suhcrom tried to reason with him. But Suhcrom was his older brother, so Naddih decided he could trust him on this one — this time.

"Now, if you don't say a word to Enomih or Jomfeh, we'll be fine," instructed Suhcrom as he flushed the toilet. *Swoooosh!* "And if they ask where the new roll of toilet paper is, just say it fell into the toilet when you were rolling it off. So you tossed it in the garbage."

"But why do I have to take the blame?"

"Because you're younger and more believable. I can't lie; they'd never believe me. I sweat too much when I lie."

The boys stared with curiosity as the water gradually swirled the mound of twisted tissue. Slowly, slowly it churned, mixing it into a watery glob. Then, it sank like a lead balloon. The paper sat there at the bottom of the bowl in a giant blob plugging the toilet. *Blub...blub, blub....*

"Uh-oh," moaned Suhcrom. *"Naddih, quick, stick yu hand in deh and grab di tissue!"*

"Who, me?"

"Yea, grab it. Quick! *Di waata is comin' up.*"

"No way. Why don't you grab it, Mr. Boss Man. I'm not putting my hand in no toilet," Naddih whispered, shaking his head. He cast a disgusting look at Suhcrom and slowly backed away.

"Why not?" Suhcrom glared at his brother.

"Didn't you use it earlier today?" Naddih asked.

"So what if I did? Come on, man, grab di tissue before it floods."

*Swoooosh!* Naddih hit the handle again.

"Uh-oh, Suhcrom, Suhcrom, *di waata is comin' up. Di waata is comin' up,*" yelled Naddih.

"Oh *maaan*, quick, get the plunger, Naddih." Suhcrom didn't know whether to laugh or cry.

Naddih grabbed the plunger that was kept at the side of the toilet. The water was spilling out all over. And while Naddih plunged with all of his strength, Suhcrom reached for some nearby towels to mop up the sloppy mess on the floor. Suddenly they heard a *knock,*

*knock, knock* at the door. They both drew in a breath and stood still. Suhcrom put his finger to his lips, signaling to Naddih to keep quiet.

*"Hey, unu betta be bathin' in deh, nuh jus turnin' on di waata and pretending to wash yu body,"* Enomih hollered. *"And no leave di towels pon di floor."*

She tried to open the door, but it was locked. *Bam! Bam! Bam!* She pounded on the door a second time. *"A weh unu lock di door fa? Open it before mi kick it down!"*

"Holy Cow, she's gonna beat the door down!" Suhcrom whispered, holding back his laughter.

*"Unu betta bathe gud…and mi seh no leave di towels pon di floor,"* she yelled.

"Leave us alone. Just let us be!" Naddih shouted. He let out a tiny giggle, and then quickly covered his mouth.

"Oh you two troublemakers," Enomih mumbled. She pounded her heels into the floor as she stomped away.

As soon as they were sure she was gone, they finished the task at hand. Naddih continued to plunge until finally the toilet emptied. Suhcrom sopped up the rest of the water and hid the wadded up towels on the floor behind the toilet. Slowly they opened the door. Naddih looked both ways. They scampered out of the bathroom with the empty toilet paper rolls and quickly resumed their project.

The boys had to move fast. Suhcrom found the matchboxes and got the crazy glue from their father's carpentry box. Naddih observed as Suhcrom glued the two cardboard toilet paper rolls to the matchbox and taped clear plastic wrap over the open ends of the rolls. It came together perfectly.

"Look at these, Naddih. Wow, aren't they awesome?" Suhcrom proudly exclaimed. He held them on display for Naddih to view.

"Let me see them, let me see them! I want to try them out." Naddih held them up to his eyes and pretended to search the room. "Oh yes, Suhcrom, these are a great pair of binoculars. We will be stylin' and wildin'. We're going to be able to search the desert for other nomads now. We'll be able to see for miles!"

"Not bad, huh?" Suhcrom puffed out his chest. He tucked his hands into his pockets and nodded his head. A contented grin spread from ear to ear.

The two boys ran outside and quickly hid the binoculars under the tent for the next day's journey. They got back into the house just as their father was walking through the other door.

"That was close," Suhcrom muttered under his breath. He wiped the sweat off his brow.

Suhcrom glanced at Naddih. It was like they read

each other's minds. They both immediately understood what the other was thinking—they needed to keep their mouths shut. Being nomads had to be kept a secret at all costs!

So they both grabbed their schoolbooks and quickly sat down in the living room. They knew how much it would please their father to see them studying, especially during the summer. He had always encouraged them to do well in school. "Education is important. You will need it in the future to better provide for yourselves and your families," he always told them.

Most of the time Jomfeh's words seemed like jibber-jabber to Suhcrom. He was really only interested in playing soccer and having some fun. However, Suhcrom and Naddih both knew this moment was critical to their secret; so they opened their books and started to read.

The minute Jomfeh witnessed the suspicious scene in the living room, he knew something was up. These boys *never* voluntarily studied, especially in the summer. Something was brewing with these mischievous little rapscallions! So he decided it was time for one of his infamous pop quizzes.

"Okay, Suhcrom. Take your book, *The Tortoise and the Hare*. Begin reading out loud," Jomfeh said sternly. "You too, Naddih, get your book."

*Oh, maaan, not a pop quiz!* Suhcrom thought to himself. He started sweating from everywhere—from behind his ears, down the front of his neck, to the palms of his hands and the soles of his feet.

"Huh? Do you mean right now?" Suhcrom asked. "Because I'm not finished with this chapter yet, Jomfeh."

"Begin reading," Jomfeh repeated. He nodded at Suhcrom.

"Uh-hmm," Suhcrom coughed and cleared his throat. He wiggled around to get comfortable on the couch. As he stared at the page in front of him, he quickly scanned the words. He repeated them over and over and over in his head so he would get them right. His father sat beside him patiently waiting. But as he began, he got stuck on the very first word.

"*Pr...aps,*" Suhcrom said as he started shaking like a leaf. He'd messed it up. "*Par...aps,*" he kept trying, but he just couldn't seem to get it right. After a number of failed attempts, his father pronounced it for him.

"Perhaps," Jomfeh said calmly. "Now, try it again."

"*Pru-hops,*" Suhcrom attempted again. Giant beads of sweat dripped off his forehead.

"*P-e-r-h-a-p-s,*" Jomfeh repeated slowly. "Say it again until you get it right."

In spite of his father's coaching, Suhcrom just couldn't

say the word correctly. He was really struggling. His shirt was soaked through, and the pages of the book were damp with sweat. Eventually, his father took pity on him and decided to let him off the hook.

"All right, Suhcrom. That is enough for now. But you need to continue with your reading until you're able to pronounce your words correctly, understood?"

Suhcrom nodded; his shoulders slumped and his head dropped to his chest.

Motionless and wide-eyed, Naddih had been watching silently as Suhcrom suffered through his ordeal. He was sweating, too, as he sat on the couch waiting his turn. *Oh, man, I just know he's going to ask me to do spelling!*

"Okay boys. That will be all for now," Jomfeh said as he got up off the couch. "Continue with your reading until supper is ready." He left the room, satisfied that both boys knew they'd been found out.

Suhcrom looked up and cast an evil look towards Naddih.

*"How mi hav fi read and yu no hav fi read?"* Suhcrom complained. *"Dat no right."*

Naddih shrugged his shoulders. He didn't know. Nor did he care. He was just relieved to have escaped a pop quiz.

Meanwhile, Enomih was in the kitchen cooking. The aroma of jerk chicken and fried plantains filled the room. When supper was ready, they all sat down together. They chatted back and forth about this thing and that—nothing of any great significance, and certainly, to Suhcrom and Naddih, nothing even close to the excitement of their nomad adventure that day. Enomih and Jomfeh still had no idea. These boys had pulled off their nomad scheme right under their very noses!

*"Suhcrom and Naddih, a weh unu du fi di wul day?"* Jomfeh asked.

"Oh, not much," Suhcrom responded. He shifted his eyes away from his father and took a bite of chicken. "We just hung around, played a bit, stuff like that."

It was really hard to stay cool, calm, and collected. Already Jomfeh had figured out they hadn't been studying. They hadn't fooled him for a minute! Suhcrom figured he'd said enough.

"Yea, we just wan...wan...wan..." Naddih stuttered.

Suhcrom narrowed his eyes as he silently shot daggers across the table at Naddih. He stared straight into his eyes, his expression cold as stone. *Oh, Naddih, don't you dare say anything. Don't give away our secret. Please...please...please. One word and I'll wring your skinny little neck!*

Naddih caught Suhcrom's glare. "Umm, yea, we uh, just wanted to hang around today, play outside... yeh."

Suhcrom breathed out a huge sigh of relief.

As they continued to eat, an awesome idea came to Suhcrom. They were going to need food for the next day's nomad adventure. And this time they weren't going to forget it! As supper was finishing, Suhcrom motioned to Naddih. He pointed at the leftover plantains and cupped his hand around his mouth.

"Save some for tomorrow," he whispered.

Naddih had *just* taken another bite of plantains. He immediately stopped chewing, and with his mouth wide open, he pointed to the slimy, mushy goop on his tongue.

*"Thave thome of dis fa tommawow?"* he asked. He quickly ran into the kitchen and spit out the plantains onto a piece of bread.

Suhcrom ran after him. *"A weh yu a do? Yu mus be crazy, man!* We can't use that for our sandwiches!" Suhcrom gagged. "That's disgusting!"

"But you said to save some for tomorrow."

"Yes, but I meant the ones on your plate, Naddih, not the chewed up ones in your mouth," exclaimed Suhcrom. "That is so gross."

Suhcrom grabbed the leftover plantains off the plate and made sandwiches for the next day. He thought it best to hide them in the refrigerator, way in the back of the bottom drawer, underneath all of the potatoes, onions, tomatoes, and mangos. That way no one else would see them—or eat them.

"Look here, Suhcrom," Naddih said. He grabbed the box of baking soda. "Shouldn't we sprinkle some of this on there too; you know, to kind of *camelfledge* it?"

"No, man, we're not going to be *camelfledging* anything with baking soda. It'll mess up the food, silly!" Suhcrom shook his head and sighed. "Hurry up, close the refrigerator door. Tomorrow we'll take our sandwiches with us," Suhcrom whispered.

"Okay." Naddih drilled his finger into his forehead. "I hope we don't forget!"

That's why I just told you, Naddih. It's your job to remember."

"And it's your job to remind me," Naddih quipped. "So, if I forget, it's your fault."

"Yeh, yeh, whatever—now shut the door, man. You're letting out all of the cold air."

Later that night, as they lay in bed, the nomads talked quietly back and forth about all of the exciting things that had happened that day.

"*Oh maaan*, Suhcrom, that was so funny when we were chasing the tent. The way the wind kept blowing it all over...I thought we'd never catch it!" Naddih began to giggle. "And I thought for sure I'd lose my pants. Oh my goodness...."

"Yeh, you looked really funny," Suhcrom chuckled.

As they recounted all of the crazy, silly moments, they began to live them all over again. Naddih couldn't stop talking about how ridiculous he must have looked with his pants twisted around his knees. He started giggling louder and quickly covered his mouth to muffle the laughter. This made Suhcrom giggle louder, too; and before long, they were both in tears, snorting and wheezing hysterically. They laughed so loud they had to stuff their faces in their pillows so Jomfeh and Enomih wouldn't hear them!

"When I was sliding down the hill, my shorts...my shorts, ha-ha-ha...were jammed up under my armpits. Ha-ha-ha...I was losing my grip fast. You got me just in time, Suhcrom. I don't think I could've held on much longer. Ahh...we had so much fun, didn't we?"

"Yeh, we sure did, Naddih. It was the greatest nomad adventure...the absolute best!"

"You know what was weird, though, Suhcrom? When you pulled me up to the top of the hill, my feet dragged through the dirt, and I remember thinking how good that cool dirt felt on my aching, scorched feet. Wasn't that a strange thing to think about?"

Suhcrom smirked. "So, tomorrow do you want to ride a camel?"

"Yah, mon—if you can make one!"

The exciting memories of the day lingered in their dreams as they both fell into a restless sleep. Suhcrom drifted in and out of his slumber. He tossed and turned and dreamed about the gusty winds blowing across the desert.

Then, in the middle of the night, a strange noise awakened him out of his dream. He heard Naddih moaning and groaning, thrashing around, and tossing from side to side. The groaning grew louder and louder; and then suddenly, Naddih bolted straight up out of his bed. He bounded over to Suhcrom with his arms flailing wildly in the air.

"To the hill! To the hill! To the bloody hill!" Naddih screamed.

Suhcrom was startled at first, but then burst out laughing.

"Naddih, Naddih, go back to bed, man. Go back to bed. You're sleepwalking again."

Naddih stopped dead in his tracks.

"*Yah mon*, go back to bed now. We need to get some sleep," Suhcrom repeated softly.

Naddih did an about-face and obediently returned to his bed.

"Sleep well now, Naddih. Tomorrow will be another exciting nomad day," Suhcrom whispered.

No sooner had Suhcrom finished speaking when the two of them fell sound asleep.

# CHAPTER 8

# No Bad Superheroes

The next morning, the boys got up early to eat breakfast with their father. He still had no clue about the nomad adventure. To him it was a day like any other day. Suhcrom, though, was already thinking ahead. He and Naddih had their sandwiches made for today, but they were going to need food for tomorrow. So during breakfast Suhcrom cast a glance at Naddih. Naddih understood. They would each save some plantains from breakfast to make sandwiches for the next day. It was a great plan. As soon as their father left for work, the two boys got going on their plans. It promised to be another exciting day for these nomads from Palmerston Close!

"Suhcrom, what about the knife? We need our nomad knife today," Naddih reminded.

"*Mi know, mi know*, Naddih. I had to wait for Jomfeh to leave. I'll go get it out of the toolbox now." Suhcrom started toward the closet where the toolbox was kept.

"Wait a minute, Suhcrom, are you sure about this?" Naddih winced. His stomach churned. Beads of sweat broke out across his forehead and suddenly he had a bitter taste in the back of his throat. "Jomfeh will be *SO* mad...."

"It will be fine. He'll never know—unless you go and tell him. You can't breathe a single word about this, you understand? Not one word." Suhcrom got the knife and slid it into his back pocket.

It was getting late and Enomih would be waking up soon. Quickly they packed their sandwiches, filled a soda bottle with water, and tiptoed cautiously out of the house. They crept quietly out to the coconut tree to retrieve the tent. The special nomad binoculars still lay under the tent where they'd left them the night before.

"Who's going to carry the binoculars?" asked Naddih.

"I'll carry them," Suhcrom said. "You carry the water and the sandwiches."

"Huh?" Naddih huffed. "How am I supposed to hang on to the sandwiches *AND* the water *AND* hold the tent, too? That's too much."

*"A weh yu a complain 'bout, man?* Don't be such a whiner. Why don't you carry the stuff in the crocus bag? You think you could handle that?"

"I guess...if it's not too heavy," Naddih snickered.

"I have another idea, too. What if we wrap some string around the tent? That way we'll both be able to hold it better," said Suhcrom. "And we'll be able to use the string to pull the tent up the hill."

Naddih's eyes lit up. "That's a great idea, Suhcrom. I'll go get the string."

Naddih ran into the house to see what he could find. Within minutes he returned...but not with string. Instead, he had a handful of shoelaces. Right away, Suhcrom recognized some of the laces. He stomped his foot into the dirt and clenched his jaw.

"Naddih, you were supposed to get string, not shoelaces. *Dem laces ya a from mi shoes, mi kickas—mi bes sneakas from America.*" Suhcrom dangled the laces in front of Naddih's face. "And what about these other ones? Where did they come from?"

"I'm sorry, Suhcrom. I couldn't find any string, so I just hurried and grabbed whatever I could find," Naddih replied.

He looked away from Suhcrom and sighed. He knew in his heart he had intentionally taken the laces from Suhcrom's sneakers, and from Jomfeh's shoes, too. Yet he had purposely not taken any from his own shoes. Naddih *never* wore his shoes without laces.

Suhcrom was in a rush to wrap the tent, so he decided to use the shoelaces. All the while, though, he realized it all made sense now. Jomfeh had always complained about his shoelaces missing, and Naddih always denied having anything to do with it. The truth was finally out. Suhcrom now knew who the "shoelace bandit" was. That boy was shrewd.

Recognizing there was no time to argue about this, Suhcrom tied the laces together to make a long string. He used Jomfeh's knife to make a couple small holes in the cardboard, threaded the laces through, and secured them tightly.

"Ahh...there, that should do it. We shouldn't have *any* problem carrying this tent now, Naddih. Not even if there is a big gust of wind like yesterday," Suhcrom exclaimed. *"Mi no waa fi go trough dat again!"*

This time, the trip seemed to go more quickly. It was partly because they were better prepared with supplies, and partly because they were more experienced nomads today. Once again, they had been quiet enough to escape the house without waking Enomih. She never paid that much attention to them. Plus, she was too preoccupied with her friends to really care what they did during the day anyway.

The nomads hadn't worried about sneaking past the neighbors today, either. They knew what they had to do to get through town unnoticed, and they just went about their way. They were down the street, across the field, and up the hill in no time flat! Thankfully, there hadn't been any major gusts of wind to deal with as they crossed the field, and since Naddih had worn better fitting pants today, the climb up the hill had been much easier, too.

It was still early when they reached the top of the hill. The sun shone brightly, a beautiful morning. The boys quickly set up the tent and got settled in. They had the whole day ahead of them to enjoy the spectacular view of the desert.

"Hey, Suhcrom, that was a great idea putting that string on the tent. It made it a lot easier to pull it up the hill," Naddih said.

"Yes, it sure did, didn't it?" Suhcrom replied proudly.

"Suhcrom, get the binoculars. Let's see if we can see any other nomads wandering around out there," Naddih said anxiously.

"Sure. Let's try them out and see how they work." Suhcrom reached for the binoculars and lifted them up to his eyes.

"Be careful, Suhcrom, be careful. They're very fragile."

*"Mi know, mi know. Mi nuh stupid, Naddih."* Suhcrom peered through the binoculars, scanning the desert below for any signs life.

Naddih jiggled and fidgeted next to Suhcrom. "Do

you see anything? Tell me, tell me. What do you see, Suhcrom?" he asked anxiously.

"Nuttin' yet."

"Let me look. Come on, let me check it out."

Naddih took the binoculars from Suhcrom. He searched the entire breadth of the desert, moving in a sweeping motion, turning slowly and deliberately from side to side, left to right. He gasped.

"Suhcrom, Suhcrom, I see some nomads! Look, way over yonder, due east, about 4.2897 kilometers."

Suhcrom chuckled. "Oh you do, do you?"

"Yes." Naddih peered through the binoculars again. "Wait, it looks like they've found an oasis. They're letting the camels and sheep rest." Naddih stared for what seemed to be minutes. "Yep, I knew it. They're getting their supplies out and putting up their tents. They're definitely setting up camp. And they're making a fire, too."

"I see," said Suhcrom, pretending to play along. "A fire, huh?" He laughed and looked out into the distance. He could see it in his mind. He pictured everything Naddih described. What a character that boy was. He sure could stretch his imagination. And he sure knew how to tell a good story!

"Do you think they have binoculars, Suhcrom? I bet they do. I wonder if they can see us up here."

The two nomads carried on and on. They had a grand time imagining what the other nomads were doing and wondering where they might be going next. Morning grew into afternoon as these silly boys continued talking for hours, nonstop. Suddenly both boys realized how hungry they were.

"Let's get some wood, Suhcrom," said Naddih.

"Wood? What do we need wood for?" asked Suhcrom. He glanced over at Naddih. The grin on Naddih's face gave him inklings of where he might be going with this.

"Well, now that our fellow nomads out yonder have settled in and made a fire for their supper, we should do the same. I'm starving! Let's make a fire to warm our plantain sandwiches."

"Okay, Naddih, a real fire or pretend fire?" Suhcrom asked with a smirk.

"Umm...." Before Naddih could even respond, Suhcrom interrupted him.

"Do you mean a real fire? You know, like the kind that burns, and when you put your hand over it, you cry out, 'Ooweee, that's hot!'" Suhcrom snickered.

Naddih's face lit up brighter than a peenywally on steroids. He was thrilled that Suhcrom seemed interested in his suggestion. Well, at least he didn't protest or give him a parental lecture.

"So where will we build the fire, Naddih? And how will we start it? We don't have any matches."

Naddih bobbed his head up and down. He stared into Suhcrom's eyes as a crooked grin spread across his face. "No worry 'bout it, man. I got it covered." Naddih pointed to the matchbox they'd used to make the nomad binoculars. "We have matches, Suhcrom...lots and lots of matches."

Naddih rubbed his hands together, threw his head back and laughed with a vicious roar as he flicked the box open. The matches spilled out all over the floor of the tent. They went everywhere.

"Hey Suhcrom, you know what that just reminded me of?"

"No, what?"

"Mr. Vincenzo's broken taffy machine. Remember how we banged on it and the taffy came spilling out all over the floor? Ha-ha, there was a ton of it all over the place. All the kids were scoopin' it up into their pockets."

"You remember the strangest things, Naddih."

"So where do you think we should build our fire? Maybe we can have it right here inside our tent, just like the nomads did in the *doctamentry.*"

"Naddih, I think you have your shows mixed up. Those nomads didn't build a fire inside their tent. That's crazy, man. They would have set the tent on fire! You must be thinking of the Eskimos. They built a fire inside their igloos, remember? They're in Alaska where it's freezing cold. That's the only way they can stay warm. Besides, we can't build a fire in our tent."

"Why not?" Naddih questioned.

"Uh...because we are lying on a cardboard box, that's why. We'd go up in flames!"

"Oh, yeh. That could be a problem, Suhcrom. Why don't we build a pretend fire then, and we can pretend it's cold outside...and...and, and then we can warm up our sandwiches...and, and we can pretend to make tea to have with our sandwiches and...."

Suhcrom held his stomach. He rolled around in hysterical laughter. "Slow down, Naddih, take it easy. We will build a pretend fire. It's a great idea."

Naddih got out the sandwiches. He pretended to warm them by the fire and imagined there was water boiling for tea.

*"Whrrrr, whrrrr,"* Naddih whistled. *"Di waata a boil. Grab di kettle, di waata a boil!*

"Pour me a cup of *cerasse* tea please, Suhcrom," said Naddih in his best attempt at a British accent.

"Of course, mi lord," Suhcrom replied with his British accent. He spoke to Naddih as if he were serving the

King of England. "Here is your *cerasse* tea and plantain sandwich."

Suhcrom extended his hand, pretending to hand Naddih a cup. He thought Naddih was a little delirious, though, asking for *cerasse* tea. *Cerasse* tastes really bitter. Their grandmother, whom they affectionately called Mama, always made them drink it before they returned to school in the fall. They didn't like it. But it was her tradition. She told them, *"Cerasse will clean yu blood and clear yu head. It gud fi di wul body."*

Naddih slowly rubbed his stomach. Suddenly he changed his mind.

"Hey, Suhcrom, could we make believe its *milo* instead of *cerasse? Because mi no like cerasse. Blaaaah, it mek mi belly hurt. Mi want milo."*

They both chuckled about the fictitious fire and tea. But they were eating their sandwiches. Those were real! They didn't have to fantasize about that.

These two silly nomads seemed to settle in like their fellow friends out in the desert below. As they ate, they acted out all of the things they had dreamed about doing as nomads. Their imaginations went wild! They talked and talked, covering everything from wandering across deserts to searching for an oasis; from riding camels over the huge sand dunes to herding sheep from one place to another.

They talked about how lucky they were to have binoculars and how they would use the knife. Most importantly, they made plans about where they would travel next.

As they took the last few bites of their sandwiches, they began to feel a little lazy. With their bellies full, it was time to kick back and relax. Then, as they lay there talking, their conversation changed course. The great nomad adventures were put aside as they shifted to the everyday ordinary nonsense between two silly young brothers.

"So, Naddih, which Superhero would you want to be if you had the chance? Remember, I am going to be Superman."

"No, Suhcrom, I want to be Superman."

"Naddih, you can't be Superman because I'm already Superman."

Naddih frowned. "You always take the good ones and leave me the bad ones!"

"That's not true. There are a lot of good superheroes left, Naddih...like Batman and Robin, or Aquaman. And what about Tarzan or Captain America? Those are great ones. And He-Man, Transformers, the Joker...."

"The Joker is no superhero, Suhcrom. *Him fool-fool.* He's evil. He laughs too much and is scary looking!"

"Yeh, yeh, okay Naddih, you're right. That's my mistake. Now pick one of the others."

"Maybe I will be He-Man," Naddih exclaimed. "But who is going to be the timid cat?" Naddih raised his eyebrows and looked at Suhcrom with one of his wide-mouthed grins.

Suhcrom curled his upper lip. "Oh no, don't look at me, man. I'm not gonna to be no silly timid cat."

"Then I'll be a Transformer. And, I'll transform into a military aircraft, and I'll kill off Megatron and all of his evil Decepticons," declared Naddih.

Once they settled the superhero question, there was a lull in the conversation. They both lay there in the tent, propped up on their elbows; their heads rested in the palms of their hands. They quietly stared out across the field. It was so peaceful listening to the *chirp, chirp, chirp* and *tweet, tweet, tweet* of all the summer birds. *Caw...Caw...*the faint sound of the crows could be heard as they circled around in the sky above them.

"Hey Naddih," Suhcrom asked quietly.

"Yes," mumbled Naddih.

"Hey Naddih," Suhcrom said a little more loudly.

"Yes."

"Hey Naddih," Suhcrom yelled jokingly.

"Yes, yes, Suhcrom!" Naddih yelled back with exasperation.

Suhcrom rolled over on his back. He burst into full-bellied laughter.

"Why are you doing that?" asked Naddih. He scowled. "You're teasing me. I heard you the first time."

"You do that to me all the time, man, all the time. So now you know how it feels."

"That's not fair, Suhcrom, because you know I have an ailment that makes me stutter and...and repeat myself."

"Ha!" Suhcrom laughed again. "Don't be ridiculous. You don't have any ailment. You're fine. You're just young, Naddih, that's all. Just young."

The moments passed. The nomads grew groggy from the sweltering, summer afternoon heat. Absorbed in their own private thoughts, they drifted off into a trance. They lay there quietly, until Naddih broke the silence.

"Suhcrom," Naddih said softly.

"Yes," replied Suhcrom.

"Suhcrom," Naddih repeated.

"Yes, Naddih, what is it? You're doing it again!"

Naddih looked puzzled. "What? What am I doing?" he asked.

Suhcrom blew out a big huff of air. "You're calling my name two or three times before you ask me a question. It's annoying, Naddih. Just say my name once, and when I say 'yes,' then ask me your question."

"Okay, Suhcrom, okay. Sorry." Naddih paused. "Can I ask my question now?"

"Yes."

"Was it *Caneya* and *Amewica* that Mikal and Benton went to?"

"Yes, and it's Canada and America. But what does that have to do with anything, Naddih?"

Naddih sighed. "Nuttin'. I was just thinking to myself."

"But Naddih, if you're thinking to yourself, you don't have to say it out loud. I don't always need to hear what you are thinking."

"What do you mean, Suhcrom?"

"Oh, never mind Naddih. It isn't important. Just forget it."

*VROOOOOOM!* They heard the roars of a jet engine as a plane flew over the top of their tent. At exactly the same time, Suhcrom and Naddih tipped their heads and looked up toward the sky. The plane had just taken off from the airport. It was still flying low — so low, in fact, it seemed they could almost reach out and touch it.

"We should be on that plane, Suhcrom. Maybe it's going to *Amewica*."

"It's America, Naddih, and yes, maybe it is. Wouldn't it be wonderful to go to America someday?" Suhcrom said pensively.

The boys had always dreamed of going to America to live. Jomfeh had talked with them about it a number of times; they all truly believed that one day they would actually get to move there.

"That would be a dream come true, Suhcrom. Just imagine...us, living in such a wonderful place...where the sidewalks are littered with candy and million dollar bills. Holy Smackaroni!"

"Ha-ha-ha! Yeh, and the streets are paved with gold, too," added Suhcrom. "I hear everyone there is rich and never has to work. We would live like kings."

"What if we could fly there in our tent, Suhcrom? Like we were on a magic carpet ride," exclaimed Naddih.

"Okay, let's go to America now," said Suhcrom.

"Now?"

"Yea, let's go now...........okay, we're back!"

"Back? So quick? Mi not even see it!"

Suhcrom burst out laughing and gave Naddih a teasing rub on the head. "You missed it. It was great, ha-ha-ha."

Dreams of going to America whimsically danced around in their heads, but the thought of living in such luxury was really little more than just a fantasy right now. And that fantasy was suddenly interrupted when the wind picked up. They glanced at each other.

"Here it comes again," shouted Naddih.

No sooner had Naddih spoken when the powerful gale ripped the tent out from underneath both of them, sending their tired, hot little bodies tumbling head first down the dirt hill. *He-he! Ha-ha!* Bursts of laughter faintly escaped as the boys rolled and bounced down the hill like rubber balls. The cardboard box danced in the wind around their heads.

Suhcrom landed at the bottom first, striking the side of his head against a small rock in the field. He was a little dazed, but unshaken. When he sat up, his gaze fell on Naddih. Suhcrom watched as Naddih transformed from a tumbling roll into a double flip and then into a somersault. Incredibly, Naddih landed with his feet firmly on the ground and in a full-speed run. He headed straight towards Suhcrom.

"Suhcrom, Suhcrom, are you all right? Are you all right?" Naddih shouted with concern.

"Yes, yes, I'm fine. I have a few bumps here and there. I'll be okay," Suhcrom replied. He spit out a mouth full of dirt, and then smiled at Naddih with one of his crooked-mouthed grins.

"What is it, Suhcrom? Why are you looking at me that way?" wondered Naddih.

"Man, you should have seen how you came down

that hill. I couldn't believe my eyes. You were doing somersaults, and flips, and all kinds of stuff. How'd you do that? Holy Moly, like you were a Ninja or something. *Maaan!* It was the most amazing thing I ever saw."

They laughed and laughed at how much fun their entire adventure had been, one crazy event after another. Suhcrom picked himself up off the ground and dusted himself off.

"Suhcrom, our tent is ruined…it's too ripped to use again," Naddih said sadly.

*"Mi know, mi know…."*

"Does that mean we have to go home now?"

"Well, I don't know about you, but after that tumble, I'm not climbing back up that hill again…especially if we don't have a tent."

"Yeh, good point Suhcrom. I'm pretty tired, anyway. Being nomads is hard work."

"Yes," replied Suhcrom. "And besides, we can't be nomads without our tent."

*"At leas mi pants still deh pon mi,"* Naddih giggled.

So, after all was said and done, the boys decided they had probably experienced all there was to being nomads. The idea of wandering the desert was growing old, the novelty wearing thin. With deep sighs, they mutually came to the conclusion that it was time to give up being nomads. They had lost their prized tent, and the special binoculars were nowhere to be found. They were filthy, hot, and frankly exhausted from their travels over the past two days.

"*Yah, mon,* let's go. It's time to go home," Suhcrom sighed.

"Suhcrom, what about Jomfeh's knife? Where's Jomfeh's knife?" Naddih's voice quivered. "We have to find it. We can't go home without it."

They both searched the area around them. Naddih spotted it on the ground, next to where Suhcrom had landed. He picked it up, extremely relieved it was not lost. As he hugged the handle of the knife, he raised his arm and pointed the blade towards the sky. A beam of sunlight caught the shiny tip, creating a brilliant fiery glow.

*Zzzzzzzzzzz! Zzzzzzzzzzz!*

"Something's happening, Suhcrom," Naddih said as he stood still, his mouth gaped open. A mysterious electrical current pulsated from the blade through the handle. *Zzzzzzzzzzz!* His hand quivered. He could feel the current surge all the way up his arm and throughout his whole body. Naddih's jaw dropped. Clumps of mud hung from his pearly whites. Suddenly, his dirt-covered face lit up with the biggest, broadest smile Suhcrom had ever seen. Naddih beamed from ear to ear.

"Suhcrom, Suhcrom, I just had the most amazing idea," shouted Naddih.

"What, what is it?"

"I know what we can do...we can be ninjas!"

"Yes. Yes. *EEEEEYES,*" Suhcrom belted out. His eyes lit up with delight. He looked at his younger brother in amazement. "That is an absolutely brilliant idea, Naddih." He was instantly re-energized. Naddih's vivid imagination had once again saved the day!

Naddih's mind raced with all kinds of ideas. Thoughts came so fast he couldn't stop talking about all the exciting things they could do.

They quickly ran off towards home, filled with unbridled enthusiasm. This was so exciting. They had a new plan. As they skipped and frolicked across the field, these two young brothers were already scheming about their exciting ninja adventure.

"Ha-ha! We shall be ninjas, Naddih," Suhcrom sang out exuberantly. He twirled around and around, jumped high in the air and clicked his heels.

"Yes," proclaimed Naddih, "we shall be ninjas. Silly ninjas we shall be!"

# Patois Words and Phrases

(Presented in order of appearance by chapter)

## Main Characters

Suhcrom – (SU crom)

Naddih – (NA dee)

Enomih – (ee NO mee)

Evrohl – (EV roll); also known as Jomfeh (JOM fay)

## Chapter 2 — Palmerston Close

18 *Howdy!* — Hi! or hello!

18 *How yuh a do?* — How are you doing?

18 *It's an irie day, mi fren!* — It is a great day my friend!

18 Dandy Shandy — A popular Jamaican child's game similar to American dodge ball. Instead of using a ball, they use an empty one-pint juice box stuffed with newspaper.

20 *Crocus bag* — a very large sack made of burlap cloth

21 *Luk ova desso man, shine di light ova desso.* — Look over there man, shine the light over there.

21 *Mi tink mi see a crab movin' ova desso.* — I think I see a crab moving over there.

25 *Yah mon, like di time wi a go sell Tiki Tiki to dem*

*fishermen?*—Yeh man, like the time we were going to sell Tiki Tiki to those fishermen?

25 *Tiki Tiki*—the Gambusia fish species, commonly known as 'Tiki Tiki'; they are known to feed on mosquito larvae, and thus are used to reduce the mosquito population.

## Chapter 3—The Desert Awaits

27 *Yah mon*—literally means "Yes, man"; a very commonly used phrase in Jamaica, similar to saying "Okay, man."

27 *Mi a hurry Suhcrom, but di box a slip outta mi hands.*—I am hurrying Suhcrom, but the box is slipping out of my hands.

31 *A weh yu a do? Yu crazy, man, yu crazy! Yu waa fi kill wi?*—What are you doing? You're crazy, man, you're crazy! You want to kill us?

32 *Di man was so crazy.*—That man was so crazy.

32 *A gud ting Jomfeh no know' bout it.*—It is a good thing Jomfeh doesn't know about it.

## Chapter 4—Freedom to Roam

36 *Chak'awaa bakayuh poolasseh*—Naddih's gibberish; this means absolutely nothing.

36 *A weh yu a seh, man?*—What are you saying, man?

39 *Yah mon, mi pants...mi pants a drop off....*—Yeh man, my pants...my pants were falling down.

42 *A weh yu do dat fa, man?*—What did you do that for, man?


## Chapter 5—To the Hill

42 *Poor ting*—poor thing

44 *Man, a wa dat?*—Man, what is that?

46 *Mi no know 'bout dat, man.*—I don't know about that, man.

47 *Festival*—a sweet dough made from cornmeal, flour and sugar, and fried in oil

47 *Sprat fish*—a kind of fish commonly found in Jamaica and most often cooked by frying in oil

50 *bouy*—boy

50 *Yah mon, mi no waa fi be last. Cuz mi poor little feet cyaa tek di switches, man.*—Yeh man, I don't want to be last. Cuz my poor little feet can't take the switches (sticks), man.

51 *Mi no tink nobody will get an infection, man. But wi can bury di bones.*—I don't think anybody will get an infection, man. But we can bury the bones.

51 *Mi no waa any of dem wild dogs eatin' di bones and disrespectin' mi fren, Helmet.*—I don't want any of

those wild dogs eating the bones and disrespecting my friend, Helmet.

53 *Di wind a blow dirt in mi face.* — The wind is blowing dirt in my face.

53 *Wa?* — What?

53 *Mi seh, di wind a blow dirt in mi face.* — I said the wind is blowing dirt in my face.

53 *Mi cyaa hear weh yu a seh, man.* — I can't hear what you're saying.

53 *Agh, mi no seh nuttin' man.* — Agh, I'm not saying nothing, man.

55 *No, man. No worry 'bout it.* — No man, don't worry about it.

## Chapter 6 — Camels-Binoculars-Knives

58 *A weh yu a seh, man?* — What are you saying, man?

58 *Weh yu waa wi fi do?* — What do you want us to do?

60 *Mi know, mi know* — I know, I know

62 *Mi a try, mi a try. Mi a do mi bes, man.* — I'm trying, I'm trying. I'm doing my best, man.

62 *Man, yu makin' mi hungry. Wi hav ani sandwiches?* — Man, you're making me hungry. Do we have any sandwiches?

63 *Tek a gud look pon mi back, man. Yu see a hump?* — Take a good look at my back, man. Do you see a hump?

64 *Mi see peenywallies.*—I see peenywallies (fireflies; lightning bugs).

65 *Man, stop yu nonsense. Mi no see any ting like dat.*— Man, stop your nonsense. I didn't see anything like that.

67 *Hey, weh yuh boys been?*—Hey, where have you boys been?

67 *Why yuh two so dutty?*—Why are you two so dirty?

67 *Hey, wah kinda mischievous tings yuh boys been up to?*—Hey, what kind of mischievous things have you boys been up to?

67 *Mi a go tell yuh faada!*—I'm going to tell your father!

## Chapter 7—The Nomads' Secret

69 *A weh unu been all day?*—Where have you (plural) been all day?

69 *Unu gone all day and left mi wid all di work.*—You've been gone all day and left me with all the work.

69 *Shush. Mi no waa fi hear no excuses.*—Hush. I don't want to hear any excuses.

69 *Di least unu can do is tek out di garbage.*—The least you can do is take out the garbage.

69 *Mi hav to do every ting. Unu do nuttin'.*—I have to do everything. You do nothing.

69 *Mi no know where yu been, and unu so dutty! Go bathe before wi eat.*—I don't know where you've been, and you're so dirty! Go bathe before we eat.

71 *Deh mus be one more roll in ya.*—There must be one more roll in here.

71 *Mi pants fine, man. Nuttin' wrong wid it.*—My pants are fine, man. Nothing wrong with it.

72 *Suhcrom, dis no feel right, man.*—Suhcrom, this doesn't feel right, man.

72 *Yu a go keep yuh moute shut, right?*—You're going to keep your mouth shut, right?

73 *Naddih, quick, stick yu hand in deh and grab di tissue!*—Naddih, quick, stick your hand in there and grab the tissue!

73 *Di waata a come up.*—The water is coming up.

75 *Hey, unu betta be bathin' in deh, nuh jus turnin' on di waata and pretendin' to wash yu body.*—Hey, you better be bathing in there, not just turning on the water and pretending to wash your body.

75 *And no leave di towels pon di floor.*—And don't leave the towels on the floor.

75 *A weh unu lock di door fa? Open it before mi kick it down!*—What did you lock the door for? Open it before I kick it down.

75 *Unu betta bathe gud...and mi seh no leave di towels*

*pon di floor.*—You better bathe good...and I said don't leave the towels on the floor.

79 *How mi hav fi read and yu no hav fi read?*—How come I had to read and you didn't have to read?

79 *Dat no right.*—that's not right.

80 *A weh unu du fi di wul day?*—What did you do the whole day?

81 *A weh yu a do? Yu mus be crazy, man!*—What are you doing? You must be crazy, man!

## Chapter 8—No Bad Superheroes

88 *A weh yu complain 'bout, man?*—What are you complaining about, man?

89 *Dem laces ya a from mi shoes, mi kickas—mi bes sneakas from America.*—Those laces there are from my shoes, my kickers—my best sneakers from America.

90 *Mi no waa fi go trough dat again!*—I don't want to go through that again!

91 *Mi know, mi know. Mi nuh stupid, Naddih.*—I know, I know. I'm not stupid, Naddih.

95 *Di waata a boil. Grab di kettle, di waata a boil!*—The water is boiling. Grab the kettle, the water is boiling!

95 *Cerasse tea*—a Jamaican herbal tea known for its bitterness; it is believed to be a blood cleanser and

good for preventing many illnesses such as colds, flu, headaches.

96 *Cerasse will clean yu blood and clear yu head. It gud fi di wul body.*—Cerasse will clean your blood and clear your head. It is good for the entire body.

96 *Milo*—a powder made from malted wheat or barley, and is mixed with hot or cold water to make a beverage

96 *Because mi no like cerasse. Blaaaah, it mek mi belly hurt. Mi want milo.*—Because I do not like cerasse. Blaaaah, it makes my stomach hurt. I want milo.

97 *Him fool-fool!*—He's a fool!

103 *At leas mi pants still deh pon mi.*—At least I still have my pants on.

# About the Authors

Marcus E. Mohalland was born in Jamaica and was raised in communities that, according to Jamaican standards, were in between poor and middle class. Many of his own life experiences are recounted in this story. He obtained his Master's degree from Binghamton University and resides in Vestal, N.Y. "I have always desired to write about my life in a way that would encourage youth to enjoy their childhood, be grateful for what they have, and motivate them to achieve their greatest potential."

Janet L. Lewis Zelesnikar, was born and raised in Endicott, New York. She obtained her Bachelor's degree from Syracuse University and is a Registered Nurse. She lives in Endwell, N.Y. with her husband, John, and her best furry friend, Sam. "Every child deserves to have fun as they grow and learn and should be encouraged to use their imagination. I was privileged to have such a childhood."

Visit our website at www.mohallandlewisllc.com to learn more about us and our company.

STAY TUNED...

THERE'S MORE SILLY NOMADS

COMING SOON...

**Vol. 2   Silly Nomads Go Ninja Crazy**

**Vol. 3   Silly Nomads Make Great Superheroes**

**"WI SO SILLY, MAN!"**

Made in the USA
Middletown, DE
24 January 2018